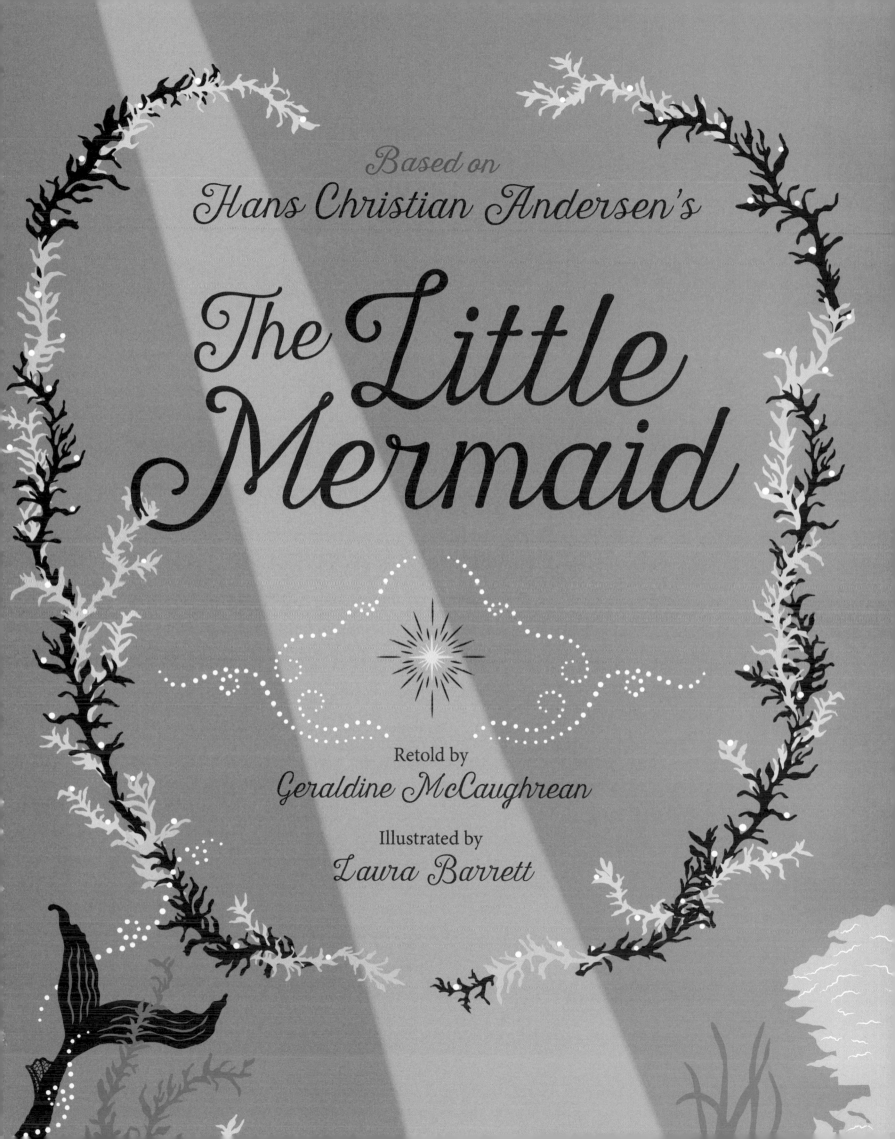

Based on
Hans Christian Andersen's

# The Little Mermaid

Retold by
Geraldine McCaughrean

Illustrated by
Laura Barrett

ORCHARD BOOKS

First published in Great Britain in 2019
by The Watts Publishing Group

10 9 8 7 6 5 4 3 2 1

Text © Geraldine McCaughrean, 2019
Illustrations © Laura Barrett, 2019

A CIP catalogue record for this book is
available from the British Library.

ISBN 978 1 40835 723 1

Printed and bound in China

An Hachette UK Company
www.hachette.co.uk

www.hachettechildrens.co.uk

Orchard Books
An imprint of Hachette Children's Group
Part of The Watts Publishing Group Limited
Carmelite House
50 Victoria Embankment
London EC4Y 0DZ

For Katy, with a Y
- L. B.

For Vivien May
- G. McC.

ORCHARD

Based on
Hans Christian Andersen's

# The Little Mermaid

Retold by
Geraldine McCaughrean

Illustrated by
Laura Barrett

# Deep down where the seaweed swish-swashes

and the sea whispers stories, lived six sisters. Mermaids.
Daughters of the Sea King. The sun and moonbeams reached
down to stroke their golden hair, but until they came of age,
none was allowed to visit the sea's surface.

In time, five of the sisters celebrated their birthdays.
Up they swam, and came back talking of such wonders
that the littlest – Delphine – ached to see the wide world above.

At last, Delphine's birthday came –
a whole day full of joy and laughter.

## Up she swam,

to be greeted by the noisy cheering of seagulls and a sunset of
red and gold. But *oh!* when she sang, sea and sky fell silent,
for Delphine had the loveliest voice of any mermaid in all the oceans.

Not far off lay a great ship, lit by lanterns and rocked by the waves.
Delphine swam closer. Another birthday was underway:
that of a young prince. There was music, laughter and
the strange sight of land-people dancing…on two legs!

Then fireworks! Starbursts of silver and glittering gold lit the
upturned faces. Delphine saw just one – the prince's.
It spun her heart like a Catherine wheel.

But that very moment, the skies rumbled, the sea shuddered.
The waves sharpened their teeth and a wicked wind blew.
Instead of fireworks, lightning blazed.
The sailors' faces shone pale with fear.

The ship put on sails and made for safety . . . *but too late*.

As Delphine watched in horror, huge waves opened their jaws
and swallowed it down.

Delphine struggled through jagged timbers and tangled ropes.
By the flare of lightning she found the prince, sinking, drowning.
Holding his sweet face between her hands, thrashing her
powerful tail, she made for land.

*That palace over there was
surely the prince's home.*

Lying in the shallows, Delphine felt his breath on her cheek,
longed for his eyes to open.

But *oh!* someone was coming! A girl on her way to the nearby harbour.

*Delphine must not be seen!
A mermaid must
never be seen!*

The girl on the beach ran straight to the prince, shouting for help.
Then she laughed out loud when he opened his eyes and smiled.

Night after night, Delphine swam back to that little cove.

She watched the palace windows – even glimpsed her prince.

But how would they ever meet again, land-man and mermaid?

Her songs became so sad that her sisters guessed her secret.

"Delphine is in love with her prince."

"Oh, she mustn't be! Land-folk think mermaids are monsters!"

"*He* wouldn't: Delphine saved his life!"

"But he doesn't realise it was her!"

"He would love her anyway. Everyone does!"

"And I love *him*," said Delphine. "I would give anything to be his wife."

"Be sensible, dearest. It can't happen. We swimmers
cannot go ashore."

Pale with fear, the littlest mermaid replied. "There is a way."

"*No!*" said her sisters. "*Not that!*"

The sea witch lives deep in the sea forest,

in a house made from the bones of drowned sailors.
Her pets are squirming sea slugs and octopuses.

But she knows Magic.

"You want to become human? Fool!" said the witch.
"Oh, I have the potion, but do you have the courage?
This magic cannot be undone. I can give you legs that dance,
but each step will hurt horribly. And if your prince gives
his heart to another, your own will shatter like a wave and
you will dissolve into seafoam. Still want my potion?"

"No!" cried her sisters.

"Yes!" said Delphine.

"Then pay my price.
I want that beautiful voice of yours."

"No!" cried her sisters.

But Delphine said nothing, for her voice
was already clutched in the claw of the sea witch,
who swallowed it down like an oyster.

Next morning, the little mermaid pulled herself out of the sea on to a
sunny rock. When she drank down the potion, pain tore into her body.
Her gleaming tail split into two long legs, goosebumpy with cold.

Cloaked in only her golden hair, balancing on frail, trembling legs,
she climbed the steps of the prince's palace.

Delphine was the loveliest person the prince had ever seen.

*"Who are you?"* he begged.

They rode together, danced together, walked in the woods.
Only the prince spoke, because Delphine could say nothing.
But her eyes spoke love with every glance.

And each night she went down to the sea, in secret,
to wash the blood from her feet.

The prince spoke often of the girl on the beach, the one
he thought had saved him. "I wish I could thank her."

Delphine mouthed a silent, *"Me! I saved you!"*

But of course he did not hear her.

No matter. Every day Delphine's eyes would speak love. Her steps would
write "Love" on the ground. She would be such a devoted friend that one
day he was sure to love her in return. That was all the thanks she wanted.

*But . . .*

"My parents want me to marry!"
wailed the prince one day.
"Some princess I have never met!
They say I must visit the girl, and try to love her!"

The news struck terror into Delphine. Her prince married?
And unhappily? Unbearable!

Suddenly the prince's face brightened. "I'll go there – but then say no
and marry you instead, dear little friend!"

And he laughed and kissed her.

Delphine's heart sang, even though she could not.

*The princess lived on the coast of a nearby kingdom.*

Delphine hoped she would be hideous and horrid . . . then unhoped it,
because she was never, ever unkind.

Sure enough, the princess was almost as lovely as Delphine.
Her face lit up when she saw the prince . . .

. . . and so did his.

For here was the very same girl who had found him
washed up on the beach and run to help him!

"I had to sail home not knowing if you had lived or died!" said the princess.

"*Marry me!*" cried the prince, to the astonishment
of kings, queens and courtiers.

"*Of course!*" cried the princess and showered him with kisses.

Delphine mouthed a silent, "*NO!*"

On the day of the wedding, Delphine danced for
bride and groom – her wedding gift.
They gasped at her graceful steps, but could not see the pain
they caused her, could not see her heart breaking. Or her fear.

Tomorrow, at dawn, her body, heart and soul must turn to seafoam
and scatter on the wind. That dance had been her last.
This scarlet sky was her final sunset. Those lovely, leaping dolphins
the last she would ever see . . .

*Wait, not dolphins, no.*
*Her mermaid sisters!*

But where were their rippling cloaks of golden hair?

The eldest held up a dagger.

"*Take it!*" she called. "We bought it from the sea witch!"

"We paid with our hair!"

"It will cut through the magic!"

"You will be a mermaid again, Delphine! Take the knife!"

"You need not die if you . . ."

"*Kill the prince!*"

Delphine took the dagger.
Overhead, the moon turned deathly pale.

Delphine's prince lay sleeping, holding his
princess in his arms, beneath the stars.

*Delphine raised the knife in both hands . . .*

*. . . then she hurled it over the ship's side.*

How could she kill her love and spill so much happiness?

The earth rolled, the stars set.
The moon sank out of sight.
The rising sun sliced a slit in the sea.
Everything was over.

*From the ship's prow, Delphine leapt . . .*

# Ah, but . . .

There are *bigger spells* than the sea witch knows.

Better spells than her garden grows.

Huge magics are mixed out of tenderness,

*Courage* and *love* and *selflessness*.

The first sun's ray to touch the sea

*Undid* the witch's sorcery.

A mermaid plunged into the waves,

*And Delphine lived on for ten thousand days!*

Down in the deep ocean, where fish-tails swish and seahorses gallop, the sun and moonbeams dangle down through the water and five mermaids plait them into their youngest sister's hair. Though they visit the surface often, they never bring home news of shipwrecks, princes or weddings, for fear they might make Delphine sad.

But somehow Delphine's fame has spread through the five oceans.
Hulking whales and porpoises, clown fish, turtles and seals break
their journeys at the Sea King's castle, hoping to hear her sing.

*For when Delphine sings,*
the coral quivers, the water shivers,
and the little hairs stand up on the neck of the manatee.
Sad and sorry, the sea witch sobs at the sweetness of the song.